Oliver's Chickens

By Lois Simmie
Pictures by Kim LaFave

A Groundwood Book
Douglas & McIntyre

TORONTO/VANCOUVER

This book is for Oliver.
And for Doris Larson, the head chicken.
L.S.

To Jeffrey, with love.
K.L.

A Groundwood Book
Douglas & McIntyre
585 Bloor Street West
Toronto, Ontario   M6G 1K5

Canadian Cataloguing in Publication Data

Simmie, Lois, 1932–
Oliver's chickens

ISBN 0–88899–139–8

I. LaFave, Kim. I. Title.

PS8587.I5505 1992   jC813'.54   C92–093521–4
PZ7.S5501 1992

Design by Michael Solomon
Printed and bound in Hong Kong
by Everbest Printing Co., Ltd.

Table of Contents

CHAPTER ONE

A Peck of Trouble

OLIVER had a flock of chickens. Nobody else
could see the chickens, but to Oliver they
were real as real. They were big brown chickens
with yellow legs and floppy red combs.

Two of them, Doris and Henrietta, always slept perched on the head and footboards of Oliver's bed, making sleepy-cheepy noises as he drifted off to sleep and whenever he turned over in the night.

The rest of the chickens slept all over Oliver's room. Edna and Mossy perched on the edge of his top dresser drawer (Oliver left it open for them), and Ruby and Lillian on the bottom one. Hilda, Violet and Kate slept on nests of Oliver's clothes, in the empty spaces on his shelves, or perched on the rod in his closet. Elsie slept in his baseball mitt.

Oliver fell asleep each night to the lullaby sounds of their soft, throaty voices. And every night Doris leaned over from her perch on Oliver's headboard and said, "Goodnight, sleep tight, don't let the weasels bite!" And then she cackled as if it was a brand-new joke she'd just thought of.

"I won't," Oliver always replied, though he wasn't the least bit afraid of weasels.

"Goodnight Doris, goodnight Henrietta," he said as he snuggled into his comforter. "G'nite Edna, g'nite Lil..." Usually he was asleep before he got all the way around.

In the morning they walked all over his room in that funny way chickens do, like they're trying to get someplace ahead of their legs. They got in his way as he dressed for school, but he was so used to it he hardly even noticed.

If he rode his bike to school, only Doris went along, riding in the basket.

"Never put all your chickens in one basket, Oliver,"she always said as she settled herself comfortably. As if he could. While they rode along, Doris sang a little song:

Oh I love the wind in my feathers
In all kinds of climates and weathers...
With my beak in the breeze
And the wind on my knees
And the *beautiful* smell of the heather!

There was no heather for a thousand miles, but Doris never worried about a little thing like that when she needed a rhyme.

Doris had a terrible singing voice, and whenever they hit a bump she squawked horribly right in the middle of a word. And she never sang a song the

same way twice. She said it was because she had a very original mind, but Oliver knew it was because she couldn't remember the words. Doris had a terrible memory.

All of the chickens gathered on the sidelines when Oliver played ball, cackling and hopping with excitement.

They cackled and hopped when he hit the ball, and when he missed it, and when he struck out. They cheered especially hard when he fell flat on his face. Oliver could never get them to understand about baseball. Once he lost a game because Edna ran out and tripped him as he rounded third base. When you aren't very good at sports, it doesn't help knowing a chicken might zip in front of you any second.

When Oliver walked to school, all the chickens went along. They settled themselves here and there around the classroom and in the coatroom on the baseball mitts. Doris's favorite spot was right on the teacher's desk. She always slept through science and math classes, but she loved the story Teacher told every day after lunch. Sometimes she got so excited she jumped right up onto Miss Frith's shoulder and peered into her ear as if she might see where the story was coming from. Of course Teacher never noticed.

One day as he watched the older boys play basketball, he saw Henrietta perched on the hoop just as someone was going to score.

"Look out! Look out for Henrietta!" he yelled just as the ball smacked her hard little head.

"Knock it off," squawked Henrietta, flapping her wings and glaring down.

"I wish he had," muttered Oliver, his face turning as red as Henrietta's comb. "Darn chickens."

The gym teacher gave him a peculiar look when he said "darn chickens." Sometimes Oliver wished he just had a pet mouse like his friend Jeremy had.

13

CHAPTER TWO

Pussywillows and Potholes

FOR a long time Oliver's parents didn't mind about the chickens. When he was really little they didn't cause too much trouble except for things like Oliver refusing to eat chicken and making an awful fuss when his mother cooked it because the chickens were all in his closet, hiding their heads under things and crying. Every so often Oliver's folks went out and stuffed themselves with Kentucky Fried Chicken.

One beautiful spring day Oliver and Doris went for a long bike ride. The warm sun shone as they rode along, and the wind ruffled Doris's rich, rust-colored feathers. She sang her new spring song at the top of her voice:

> Pretty pussywillows and potholes
> They are here every year in the spring
> With the first you can make a furry bouquet
> With the second you can't do a thing
> Oh, PUSSYwillows and pot...

THUMP! The front wheel dropped into a big hole in the road. Doris flew out of the basket tail over comb with Oliver right behind her. They hit the road in a terrible tangle and were almost run over by a car.

"That's that," said Oliver's parents after he was patched up. "If it weren't for those chickens, this wouldn't have happened."

"It wasn't Doris's fault," Oliver said.

He knew this was true, but he also knew he should have been watching the road instead of looking at the sun in Doris's feathers.

Oliver's mom and dad went into the study and shut the door. He could hear the murmur of their voices.

After a long time, Oliver's folks stopped talking and made hot dogs and beans, his favorite supper.

"We're going on a picnic tomorrow," said his father as he passed Oliver the mustard and relish.

"Oh boy, I love picnics. Where are we going?"

"To an island on Little Lake," said his mother. "Won't that be fun?"

"A real island? Can I take the chickens?"

"By all means," said his father. "Bring all of them."

"Won't it be crowded in the boat?"

"We'll manage," said his mother. And she made chocolate sundaes for dessert.

Oliver ran to tell the chickens.

"A sea voyage? How wonderful!" cried Doris. "Did I ever tell you I come from a long line of seafaring chickens?" Doris changed her ancestry to suit the occasion. "My great-great-grandfather was a sea captain."

Oliver didn't have the heart to tell her it was not the sea but a lake, and a rather small one at that. More like a pond, really.

"I will compose a sea shanty for the journey," Doris said.

CHAPTER THREE

The Voyage

THE next day they drove to Little Lake and Oliver's father rented a rowboat.

"For how many?" asked the boatman.

"Thirteen," said Oliver.

"Three people," said his father. And they all crowded in and set off for the island.

Oliver felt sorry for the chickens. They looked exceedingly gloomy, scrunched down in the bottom of the boat with their eyes closed. All except Doris, who stood on the prow with her toes hooked under a rope and her beak pointed straight ahead. It was a lovely blue boat, and the water made little smacking sounds against the sides. As Oliver's father rowed, Doris sang her sea shanty:

> I've sailed on the brine in rain and in shine
> I've sailed in the teeth of a blizzard
> For I am a nautical, *yacht*ical bird
> And sailing is in my gizzard!

"Oh Lord, she's at it again," said Henrietta, who was a bit envious of Doris's song-writing abilities. The others, who were feeling quite seasick, just moaned. Oliver held Edna and Lillian, one under each arm, and Mossy climbed onto his lap and pushed her head up under his lifejacket. They kept

him nice and warm all the way to the island.

Oliver helped his father pull the boat right up onto the sand so the chickens could hop out without getting wet. They immediately bobbed off into the bushes to explore.

Oliver and his folks took a hike around the island, which had lots of good places for chickens to roost, or have dust baths, or just wander around and peck at things.

"They like it here," said Oliver.

"Yes," said his father. "This would make a wonderful home for them, wouldn't it?"

Oliver nodded.

"I mean," said his father, "it's a much better home for chickens than a little boy's room. When you really think about it."

Oliver looked at his mother. She smiled at him the way she did when she loved him even more than usual, which was a lot.

"We would like you to think about leaving the chickens, Oliver."

"You mean leave them here."

They nodded.

"But chickens can't swim."

"No, they can't."

"They would stay here for always," Oliver said.

"Yes, they would."

"Could we maybe come and see them sometime?"

His father looked at his mother. "Yes. Sometime."

"I will have to think about it," Oliver said.

"Of course. You must think about it very carefully," said his mother.

Oliver went for a long walk. In a sunny clearing, Lillian and Mossy were tugging a worm back and forth between them.

A pine cone dropped on Oliver's head, and he looked up to see Ruby and Henrietta nestled in

the low branches of a spruce tree as if they belonged there. A fern moved, and he saw Elsie's bright eye peering out from between the fronds. Hilda and Kate were busily pecking bugs out of an old hollow log, and Violet and Edna were sound asleep in the sun in nests of long dry grass.

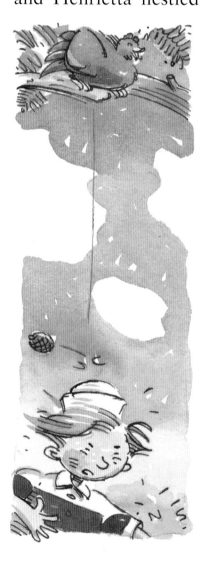

He found Doris last, pacing up and down the beach. Oliver sat down to watch her.

Back and forth she went, back and forth, with her head down, leaving chicken tracks in the hard damp sand.

"What are you thinking, Doris?" Oliver asked after awhile.

"I am thinking...something," Doris replied.

"I am too," said Oliver.

Doris looked at him. "You go first."

"Well." Oliver took a deep breath. "I am thinking that this island would make a very good home for..."

He stopped.

"For Henrietta...and Violet...and Mossy..." said Doris slowly.

"And for Edna and Kate and Hilda," said Oliver in a rush.

"And for Ruby and Elsie and Lillian," replied Doris in a more ordinary kind of way.

"And for..." Oliver stopped. He couldn't say it.

"For me," said Doris.

They were both silent for a long time as the water made small swishing sounds on the beach and the wind sighed in the pine trees.

"I think," Doris finally said, "it is for the best. It is *appropriate*." She stood tall and puffed out her chest. "Our grandparents were island chickens and we will be island chickens. We are Rhode Island Reds."

They looked at each other. Then Doris went to tell the other chickens, and Oliver went to tell his folks.

CHAPTER FOUR

The Gift

WHEN Oliver came to say goodbye, the chickens were all gathered together, clucking excitedly. All except Edna who was sleeping in a hollow stump.

Doris flapped up onto a log and held out her wings for silence. Then she began to sing:

> We're going to be island chickens now
> The way we were meant to be
> Cut off from civilization
> By the width of the raging sea...

They drew silently closer to Oliver as Doris sang:

> We're naming this Chicken Island
> And this will be Oliver's Beach
> You'll miss us all, and we'll miss you
> And that's the end of my speech.

She called it a speech so it would rhyme with beach.

Henrietta stepped forward and dropped a very large, very dead beetle at Oliver's feet.

"We will carry you in our hearts," called Henrietta as Oliver walked away with the beetle in his pocket.

"And in our gizzards!" called the other chickens.

"...in our gizzards," echoed Edna sleepily.

As the boat pulled away from the island, Oliver looked back. They were all lined up on the beach, watching him go. Even Edna, who was only half awake.

"Goodbye," Oliver called as Doris hurried down to the edge of the water.

"Goodnight, sleep tight, don't let the weasels bite!" she called, and cackled one last time. Oliver waved and turned away.

CHAPTER FIVE

Row, Row, Row Your Boat

OLIVER was very quiet as his father rowed along. His mother sat close to him. "Row, row, row your boat," she sang softly.

They were almost back to shore when a very large smile lit up Oliver's face. "Hello, Donalda," he said.

His parents looked at each other.

"Who is Donalda?" they asked together.

"This duck who just hopped into the boat, of course," said Oliver. "And look at all the others swimming behind."

Oliver's father began to row faster.

"I don't think they're going to catch up," said his mother. Oliver's father was rowing very fast now.

"Oh well," said Oliver, turning around. "I guess they're not. Ooooh, you're *wet*, Donalda."

Oliver smiled at his mother.

"Look, Mom. Look at her lovely orange feet."

THE END